First, a little bit about me. I aı
eight years old. I am also sing
own. I am working in a refrigeration company
warehouse as a dispatcher.

I am quite an ordinary person that blends well in
a crowd except for my need for B.D.S.M.,
which seems to dominate much of my thought
process. I have one particular fantasy above all
the others where I want to be a domestic slave. I
also have a strong desire to be feminine and
want to combine the two which I suppose means
I want to be a sissy maid. Perhaps I am not so
ordinary after all, these are not the fantasy of an
average person.

I suppose I could act out these fantasies by
either finding an obliging Mistress or seeing a
professional dominatrix. For me, however,
neither will quite do as my fantasy involves me
wanting to be a slave Twenty-Four Seven. I

want the fantasy to be real, where I am genuinely enslaved in a lifetime contract with no means to eradicate myself from it. It is the permanence of the situation that rocked my boat, I wanted to be totally out of control.

Of course, it is one thing to fantasise about these things and quite another to act them out for real. There are two difficulties with my fantasy, the first one is I will need to find a couple or a dominant who wants a live-in real slave. They do exist, but not on every corner. The vast majority of people in B.D.S.M., only want to act out their fantasies in controlled sessions and not looking for anything long-term or even slightly resembling a real-life situation. All most B.D.S.M., players are looking for is a temporary release from their fantasies and then they return to their day-to-day lives.

The other problem with my fantasy is becoming a 24/7/365 slave would mean giving up the way of life I have now and replacing it with something much, much more restrictive. For example, if I become a real slave it would mean I will never marry and have children. I would never own my own house, go on holiday, or travel. There would be no nights out and I will lose all control over my future. A slave's life is that of a skivvy, with long hours of toil, no days off and a life of drudgery with no end.

As time went by I would fantasise more and more about the above. The desire to become a slave overtook my life to the point where I would dream about being a lowly domestic slave several times a day.

I concluded this was something I needed to experience if only to purge my fantasies for good as I felt they were becoming destructive and anti-productive. I would also dream about being female and the two fantasies about being feminized and enslaved were inexorably mixed. One without the other fantasy didn't do it for me it was a definite mixture of the two ingredients.

These fantasies resided entirely in my mind and had done so for many years. I hadn't acted them out thus far. However, I always looked at the classified advertisements in specific magazines in case someone somewhere wanted a permanent live-in slave. I didn't think I would ever find such a request, but one day whilst reading a magazine that catered for like-minded enthusiasts, I saw an advertisement which asked for a live-in transgender slave. I got really excited when I saw this advertisement and wasted no time in sending a letter asking to be considered for the position. I didn't stop to think of the ramifications and obstacles to me becoming a slave I just had an overpowering need to apply as soon as I possibly could.

Some weeks passed and I had almost forgotten about my application and assumed my letter was in a sea of other such letters and probably would never get a reply. So, I wasn't holding out much hope, after all, hundreds of people would have also seen the advertisement apart from me and many might have been just as excited to apply for the position as I was.

Then just as I had given up all hope a letter popped through the letter box for me. I picked it up, wondering who it might be from as it was handwritten and clearly not a bill or a circular. Before opening the letter I saw the envelope had been stamped in Swaffham, Suffolk. I didn't know anyone in Swaffham and I didn't know where Swaffham was or had heard of the place before. I felt my blood pressure rise as I tore into the envelope. Then I stop short of taking out the letter from the ripped envelope. I realised probably it was a reply to my application, but by the same token, it may very well be a polite rejection.

I decided to control my excitement and fear the worst then I won't be in for such a big disappointment. The letter reads:

Dear Slave,

Thank you for your reply telling me and my husband all about yourself. We are indeed interested in your application and we would like to tell you more about the position and what we are looking for.

The position is for a transgender domestic slave who will be responsible for all household chores and sweeping and cleaning a furniture workshop where we make bespoke furniture. In the summer months, the slave will be required to help Mistress in the garden. The chosen slave will also be required for regular personal service. This is a lifetime position.

Now to tell you something about ourselves we are a couple in our forties, we have a four-bedroom house and a workshop where we make bespoke pine furniture.

Now please tell me more about yourself so we may take your application forward.

Yours sincerely,

Emma and Cy Woodstock.

I took the letter to work with me and read it over several times and when I got home I immediately set about drafting a reply. As requested I said a little more about myself and said I was very interested in the position and would like to take my application forward. I got my reply in the mailbox that same evening and waited anxiously for a reply. In just over a week I had another familiar letter with a Swaffham postal stamp mark.

I got up a bit late that morning and had to dash to the bus stop to get to work on time. I missed my breakfast and had no time to open my letter and had to take it with me to work. I had to wait on tenterhooks until tea break before I got a chance to open the letter and read it. The first letter was written by the Mistress, this was a shorter letter than the last reply which was written by the Master.

Dear Slave,

Have you any experience of being a slave and have you ever had chastisement before? Tell me have you ever been made to bend the back of a chair to take punishment?

Master Cy.

I wrote back immediately and said I had neither experience of being a slave before nor of being chastised. I began to worry, that would my lack of experience put them off of me, but on reflection, I didn't see why it should and waited once again for a reply by return of post. Once again the reply took about a week to arrive. This was the shortest correspondence so far and only had a telephone number on an otherwise blank piece of paper. There was no explanation, but clearly, I was expected to make use of it and give the couple a telephone call.

I waited a day or two as I was a bit nervous about telephoning as I was quite shy by nature and felt I would get tongue-tied and embarrass myself. However, I couldn't delay by telephone call too long or I risked this couple finding someone else to become their slave and I will, by my indecisiveness, miss the boat. So one afternoon I mustered the courage to give the couple a call. I was met by a female voice.

The lady on the other end of the phone sounded rather abrupt, even before I said who I was and why I was calling. Her manner didn't change once I explained and immediately went into Mistress mode.

"Thank you for calling. You have read our letters and I take it you understand what the role of the slave is and what you can expect from us?"

"Yes," I replied nervously.

"Good, good," she replied, still sounding officious. "How do you feel about spending the rest of your life dressed as a woman?"

"I would like that," I replied, "I want to spend my life as a female."

"And, how do you feel about doing menial work for the rest of your life?"

"The job I have now is menial," I replied, however, it wasn't true, my work may be boring and depressing, but it required some responsibility and skill and therefore could not be classed as menial. I was trying hard to say the things I presumed she wanted to hear.

"I presume you also realise you will be chastised? How do you feel about that?"

"I understand that slaves can be chastised from time to time," I replied, not knowing how else to answer that question.

"Three more questions for now and I will let you go," the woman said, "and what do you feel about never owning anything?

"I don't own anything now," I replied, which was close to the truth as I didn't have anything of any real value. Also to be truthful, I have always been a minimalist and have never put much credence into material objects. My philosophy is, that things fall to bits and lose value anyway.

"Is there anybody you wish to remain in contact with, for example, relatives?"

"No, I am estranged from family" I replied again untrue.

"Lastly, I presume you have been looking for a man?"

"Yes," I replied, but that wasn't true either. I lied several times during that one very short conversation.

"Well, that will do for now, thank you for calling," she said concluding the telephone conversation. "We shall write to you very shortly, good bye for now and we will talk more a little later."

I was reassured that the Mistress wanted to write and if she wasn't interested would have told me over the phone there and then. So, I went away pleased with myself and anxiously awaited the couple's next mailing.

Chapter Two

It was only a couple of days before I saw another familiar envelope drop at the foot of my door. I eagerly picked it up and used my left index finger as a paper-knife and tore open the envelope. Inside was a letter on a yellow leaf of paper and was written by the Mistress.

Dear Slave,

We are minded to give you a trial of two weeks to see if you are suitable to join us as our lifetime slave. First, may I inquire if you have any feminine clothes and a practical pair of shoes? How much notice do you need to give your present employers and notice on your accommodation?

Upon receipt of your reply, we will give you a date when to travel up to us and begin your trial.

Your Mistress,

Emma.

I noticed that the letters I received and the telephone conversation I made with this couple were always short, sweet and to the point. I assumed this was saving me from getting a sense of self-importance and I was applying to merely become their domestic slave, someone of little importance. I nevertheless wrote back saying I didn't have any female attire and I would need to give a month's notice for both my employer and accommodation and give notice immediately on a favourable reply. Much to my dismay, a reply was slow in coming and I began to get despondent as I thought perhaps they had changed their mind, or worse never genuine in the first place.

Nearly two weeks had passed and I resigned myself that I was not going to hear from this couple again. I had been in the habit of every morning running down the stairs to look to see if there was any post for me. But after two weeks or more of nothing in the mail, it became a futile pastime and I no longer made a special journey downstairs just to look for letters. Then one morning as I left the house to make my way to the bus stop for work, there was a letter at the foot of the door. I recognised it straight away. I put the letter in my coat pocket and ran to the bus stop. On the bus, I opened the envelope and read the content.

Dear Slave,

We would like you here for the 14th of June, this will give you ample time to give notice at your work and get your affairs in order before you join us. Don't worry about clothes or shoes, just bring yourself.

Do not come straight to the house, but call us on your arrival in Swaffham to give us time to be ready for you. If you arrive by train we will collect you from the railway station when we are ready to receive you.

Your Master and Mistress,

Cy and Emma.

I wrote back confirming our arrangement. So it was all set for me to become their slave. I didn't give up my job but instead booked two weeks' holiday in that period and neither did I give up my bedsit as I only intend to serve the trial period and then make an excuse to decline a permanent arrangement. However, I was looking forward anxiously to become a slave even unknowing to them it will only be for two weeks. It was an experience I needed to have to purge myself from wanting to be a slave in the future.

On the 14th of June, I got up at 5 am for my journey to Swaffham, Norfolk, and walked two miles to the main railway station. I took my new owners at their word and was just bringing myself and only had a toothbrush and a tube of toothpaste and some razors, nothing else. I thought there was no point in packing clothes as I will not be wearing male clothes once I arrive.

Even though I was some hours away from reaching Swaffham, I was nevertheless riddled with nerves. I ordered a return ticket to Swaffham, which involved a few changes on the route. I intended once I reach my destination to hide the return ticket in the lining of my toiletry bag.

The journey took hours and I reached Swaffham railway station at 2 pm. I was tired and now almost beside myself with nerves. I left the platform and entered the main station looking for a telephone kiosk, so I could let my Master and Mistress know I had arrived. Mobile phones existed, but they had yet to catch on, they were very expensive and only businessmen had such things. It was a busy station and a cluster of telephone boxes were all in use and I had to queue to take my turn.

I waited twenty minutes to get my turn the wait was agonising and I almost changed my mind and prepared for the journey back home. Then I decided that would be silly after taking all the trouble to come this far and it was only for a trial of two weeks. I eventually got my turn to make a call and I decided to go ahead and tell my Master and Mistress I am here in Swaffham.

Mistress answered the phone and she seemed almost surprised I called, maybe she too thought I would chicken out at the last moment.

'Okay," she said, "stay where you are. We might be a while so go and get yourself a coffee and something to eat and be outside the station at 3:30 and look out for a metallic blue Ford motorcar. If we are not there, just wait until we arrive."

I agreed and put the phone down and went back into the main station looking for the café. I ordered a coffee and two sausage rolls. I was too nervous to be hungry, but I had no idea when I might eat again, so it made sense to eat something now when I had the chance. I had to force myself to eat the food I bought as I didn't feel like eating at all. I kept glancing at my watch, the time was going slowly and I still had the better part of an hour to wait. This was torture in itself, as I was becoming more and more terrified at what was installed for me.

Three-thirty pm arrived and I stepped outside of the station and walked up to the edge of the pavement and looked left and right, but there was so far no sign of a metallic blue Ford car. I saw a vacant bench and went and sat down while I waited for my Master and Mistress to arrive. I don't know how many times I almost walked back into the station and caught the next rain home. However, I didn't succumb to temptation and steadfastly waited, sitting on the bench for my transport to arrive.

Finally, a blue metallic Ford car slowly pulled off the main road and entered the railway station as it drove towards me my heart missed a beat and my legs felt so weak, I thought I would fall into a heap on the pavement. Just before the car came level with me, I put my hand out to identify myself and the car stopped at my feet. My new Mistress rolled down the window of the passenger door and said:

"Are you looking for Emma and Cy?"

"Yes," I replied. The lady gave me a quick disapproving look up and down and replied.

"Jump in the back."

As soon as I sat down the car pulled away and rejoined the main highway. I noted the man was tall, slim and forty-something. The lady was of a similar age, not fat, but a little rounder and bigger boned than her husband. It was an agonising minute or two before anyone spoke. Mistress turned back to look at me and said:

" How was the journey up here, you have come quite a way haven't you?"

"Yes," I replied with a little croak of nerves as I cleared my throat to speak.

"Sit back and enjoy the drive, it will take us about half an hour to get home. We will drive through some nice countryside so make the most of it. We'll have a good talk about your new life when we arrive home," Mistress said, turning back to look at the road ahead. That was the last of the conversation until we arrived at the house.

Chapter Three

When we arrived at the house I was shown into the kitchen and told to take a seat while Master and Mistress sorted themselves out. Then the Mistress returned and gave me a weak smile and said:

"I am going to be nice to you today I am going to make you a cup of tea, probably the very last one I will ever brew for you, so make the most of it. Milk, sugar?" She asked.

"Just milk please," I replied.

"Let's start as we mean to go on, your reply will be Just milk please Mistress. Well," Mistress shouted, "repeat what I have just said."

"Just milk please Mistress," I recited nervously.

"Cy will be back shortly, he will want to talk to you too later on when I have finished with you. You'll be a slave to both of us in different ways, but I am the one you'll deal with most of the time as I shall be giving you your chores and inspecting your work. I shall also be the one to administer chastisement when it becomes necessary." Mistress said, looking for my reaction. She was disappointed, as I was far too nervous to give anything away in my body language apart from the sheer terror of the unknown.

Moments later I was passed a cup of tea and Mistress also sat with her cuppa and faced me. After a few sips of my tea, I saw told to strip all my clothes off. As I did so Mistress went to the cupboard and got a bin liner, but your clothes in here including your shoes, you won't need them anymore. Your old clothes can go to the charity shop when we next go into town as I am sure someone can make use of them," Mistress said passing me an opened bin liner. This was the first chink in my master plan as I now wouldn't be able to change back into male clothes at the end of the trail.

'I thought I was here for a two-week trial," I asked. "What if I decide this isn't for me, I won't have any clothes to wear home."

'It is a two-week trial for us, not for you, you have already agreed to become a lifelong slave, ' Mistress barked. "If we decide it won't work out, we will replace your clothes before you leave," she added dismissing the subject.

When I was stripped I was allowed to finish my cup of tea before being marched down a corridor to a bathroom. I was told to take my time and have a good shower and when dry return to the kitchen. I did as I was told and had a long shower, which I much needed as I did feel very grimy from such a long day on the train. I was also feeling very tired and would be glad when today is over, although I strongly suspected I wouldn't be able to sleep even when I get the opportunity.

When I finished showering, I dried myself off and returned to the kitchen. This time both Master and Mistress were sat at the kitchen table. They both turned to look as I arrived back in the room.

"I think she might do," Mistress observed, her husband nodded in agreement but remained silent. Cy finished his cup of tea and left the room, leaving me alone with Mistress.

"Sit Mistress barked pulling out a kitchen chair into the centre of the kitchen. I sat and Mistress picked up a comb and scissors off the table.

"Your hair is very boyish and short, but I will style it as best as I can and we will let it grow out and soon it will look much more feminine. Mistress sets about snipping and changing my parting from the left to the centre.

"Right that will do for now, the next step in your induction, is to get you dressed and show you your room and the rest of the house. When we have done that we will return to the kitchen for something to eat as I expect you must be starving by now. I was taken upstairs to your Mistress's bedroom.

"You're lucky, you and I are about the same size as myself, a size 16. This means you'll be able to fit into my old clothes which will save us quite an expense. When you're dressed I will also find you an old makeup bag and find you some old makeup I no longer use. I have tons of old make-up products in the bedroom, and sure to have something suitable for you," she said going to a wardrobe and flicking through the rack of clothes.

"Yes, she said approvingly," pulling out from the dozens of dresses a plain grey dress with white lace cuffs and hem. "This is suitable for our new maid. Now to find some underwear and black tights.

Once all the clothes were assembled on the bed I was left to dress and told to wait in the bedroom for Mistress's return. When she returned she looked at me and smiled.

"Yes, that looks nice," she said approvingly. There is one more touch, we need to make. She pulled two woollen white socks from a drawer and shaped them and put them in the cups of my bra. "This will do, for now, I will get you some proper silicon falsies in a few days' time. Then I sat down at the dresser and Mistress started my makeup.

"Take a special note of what I am doing, you'll be doing your own makeup in the future, this is just to show you the look we're looking for, for our new maid." When Mistress had finished I was shown the rest of the house which was huge and had six bedrooms which were rented out to holidaymakers during the season. It wasn't hard to realise why they needed a slave as they had the furniture business as well, it was a lot for just two people to manage. It wasn't hard to see my role will be that of a domestic and chambermaid.

In the kitchen, there was a little table and chair in a small alcove and I was told this is where I shall eat in the future alone. I was given a hot dinner and was told when I had finished I was to tidy away the dining room where the Master and Mistress had their food, wash up and then I may turn in as it had been a very long day for me.

Just as I was about to go to the living room and say good night and go to bed Mistress approached me with a traditional-looking windup alarm clock with two little bells on top.

She set the device to the correct time and also set the alarm feature for 5:30 am.

"This is for you," she said. "You're to be dressed, washed, shaved, made up and down here in the kitchen by 6:30 am. I shall put out a bowl and cereal for you. You may make yourself a cup of tea or coffee and be ready to begin work at 7 am. I should be up by then to give you instructions. Have a good night's sleep Rosie and I shall see you in the morning." Mistress turned to go back into the living room and then stopped to add:

"Oh, by the way, Cy apologises for not introducing himself properly to you. He will have a chat and get to know you tomorrow when he has more time." With that Mistress disappeared back into the living room and I was allowed to go to my room.

My room was probably the smallest in the entire house. It was hardly big enough for the bed, but I don't suppose I shall be spending very much time in my room so I don't suppose it really mattered. As I undressed for bed, it dawned on me, that I had been given the name already, Rosie. My new moniker was slipped into a conversation without me barely realising it. Being called Rosie will take some getting used to. I couldn't sleep at all that night it was a mixture of being overtired, excited, nervous, and sleeping in a new bed and surroundings.

All I could do was lie there and wait for the morning at least I didn't need to worry about oversleeping. Morning slowly arrived and I got up and made my way down the corridor to the bathroom and washed and shaved. Then I returned to my room and dressed and made my first attempt at applying makeup. I was too nervous to do a good job. When I was satisfied with my feeble efforts I gingerly made my way downstairs to the kitchen.

Just as Mistress had said, she had put out a bowl and next to it was a box of honey nut cereal. I found the milk in the fridge and made myself a cup of coffee. Almost on the dot of 7 am my Mistress emerged in her pink Candlewick dressing gown.

"Have you had breakfast?" she asked.

"Yes," I replied.

"Yes Mistress, I won't keep warning you the next time to fail to address me properly you'll be punished. "Right, let's get you working, first, let's take a look at you." Mistress studied my make-up.

"You'll need to work on your make-up skills. We'll have guests soon and I want you as passable as you can be. I think with a little effort and practice people will take you for the real thing. Now let's look at your hands." Mistress studied my hands getting me to turn them over several times. "I shall find you a selection of my old nail varnishes to play with. Also, when I shop next I will get you some rubber gloves as your hands will forever be in the water. Your hands will dry and chaff if you don't wear gloves and you won't be able to wear nail varnish without it pealing. Right come with me," she said, taking the lead and going up the stairs.

We walked to the top floor. On every floor there is a cupboard with cloths and cleaners, there is also a vacuum cleaner," she said opening a cupboard for me to see. You'll clean this floor before lunch. You don't need to change the beds today but you will do everything else. You'll sweep the floor in every room, clean the windows, dust and polish. When you have finished, you may come downstairs and find me," she said, turning to go back downstairs, leaving me to find what I need in the cupboard. I started to pull out the vacuum cleaner.

"A tip," Mistress shouted back from the stairwell. "Vacuum last as you'll be wiping particles of dust onto the floor as you clean." With those words of wisdom, I put the vacuum cleaner back and found myself some dusters. On this floor, there were two bedrooms and a bathroom. I was quick to realise, as the beds didn't need making today, and the bedrooms because of that, were quick and easy to clean, the bathroom, however, took a lot more work and was far more time-intensive. When I was finished, I was exhausted and was quick to realise there was still over half a day to go.

I made my way down the stair to find Mistress to report I had finished the top floor. I found her in the living room with Master.

"Just in time for lunch," Mistress said standing. The Master turned in his seat and smiled at me.

"I will have a chat after you have eaten," he said, turning back to his newspaper.

"Let's go into the kitchen," Mistress said. "I take it you have finished cleaning the top floor."

"Yes, I said, and then I remembered to quickly add Mistress. Mistress spotted the corrected error and said nothing.

"There is a meal for you in the oven, you will eat it here in the kitchen and when you have finished go and clear away the dining room, wash up and report to me in the living room." Mistress then left the room for me to get my meal out of the oven and eat it at the kitchen table. When I finished, I cleared away the plates from Master and Mistress's lunch in the dining room, wiped down the table, mopped up some crumbs on the floor then went back to the kitchen to wash up. As I busy myself with washing up the dishes, Master came into the kitchen.

"Leave that for a moment, wipe your hands and come and sit," he said, taking a seat himself at the kitchen table. I noticed he was tall and slim, quite unlike Mistress who was a big-boned and formidable-looking woman, especially in contrast to him. I wiped my hands and came and sat opposite my Master.

"We haven't had a chance to speak until now," he said. "As you have already realised most of your dealings are with your Mistress as she will allot your chores and administer any discipline that is required. You are a skivvy for your

Mistress but you are also a slave for me," he paused, waiting for any reaction, then he continued. "I will require personal services from you, you know what I mean by personal services don't you?" As I fumbled for a reply Master saved me my embarrassment by answering for me.

'I will require sexual services from you most evenings. After dinner tonight and every night hereafter you'll go to my bedroom and wait outside of the door for me to arrive. Do you understand," he said, rising from his seat.

'Yes Master," I replied.

'Good we will talk more and get to know each other better tonight after dinner," he said, smiling at me as he tapped my knee. With that Master left the kitchen for me to continue washing up. When I finished washing the dishes reported to Mistress in the living room and I wasn't too surprised when she told me to go and clean the second-floor bedrooms and bathroom. On this floor is my bedroom and the Master and Mistress each had their own bedrooms and didn't sleep together as far as I could tell. There was also an ensuite bathroom, which had a large Jacuzzi.

I presumed Mistress had checked my cleaning on the top floor and hadn't remarked on my work, so I assumed I met her standards which was a relief as I quite imagined her criticising my work constantly. So far there was no complaints. I got on with cleaning the rooms and straightening the beds. I spent an age cleaning the bathroom and Jacuzzi. I was quickly realizing the fantasy of being a maid cum slave was one thing and the reality quite something else. I realised all I was free labour. Still, I had only myself to blame, I had actively asked for this, and worst still I sought it out and

I got exactly what I had asked for. I had no one to blame but myself for my predicament.

I decided that I couldn't be a skivvy for life without anything to look forward to nothing to plan for, just day after day of never-ending drudgery. Paid maids would have at least one day off and some money to spend, but I wouldn't even have that. I quickly learned that even Sundays were not sacred, and I had to work these too just like any other day and far as long.

I decided I couldn't blame my Mistress or Master. This is what I asked for in full knowledge of what I was letting myself in for, so I decided to work out my trial period to the best of my ability and then make an excuse to leave. Two weeks isn't too long and will quickly pass and then I can put it all down to experience.

After dinner and all my chores were completed I did as I was told and went upstairs and waited outside of my Master's door. I was very nervous I didn't know what he intended to do with me. Would I like it or would I hate it, it made no difference I had to endure it whatever it might be. I stood there waiting for ages and finally, he appeared, acknowledged me with a nod and opened his door waving me in with his hand.

"We'll have a little chat sit on the end of the bed," he said, indicating where he wanted me to sit. He then sat in the only armchair in the room and looked me up and down. "How long have you wanted to dress up as a girl?" he asked.

"Since I was small," I replied. "I have always had a very strong feminine outlook."

"Is this the first time you have worn lady's clothes for any length of time?" he asked looking me up and down again.

"Yes," I replied.

"Here," Master said with conviction," you're our slave and you will be treated as a female slave at all times. I think with a little bit more effort on your part you'll look very passable, perhaps you shall when your hair had grown out more," He added as an afterthought. Come here," he demanded, pointing to the floor. "Kneel here in front of me." I did as requested and my Master stood and dropped his trousers and pants. "Come closer," he insisted. I was confronted with a very erect penis. "Well," don't just kneel there, start sucking."

I did as asked and I likened the experience to sucking a raw pork sausage. After a few moments, Master swayed back and forth, groaning as he ejaculated directly into my mouth in three or four big spurts. I had never tasted semen before and it wasn't as bad as I imagined. He then exhausted and flopped back into the armchair. After taking a moment or two to recover, he said:

"You did very well, I am pleased with you. You may go now." I got up to leave and as I went to the door Master added.

"Tomorrow we will try anal sex and will probably alternate between the two each evening so we don't get too stale." With that, I said good night and left the room. I am not sure how I felt about what had just occurred. I wouldn't have sought out sex with another male that is for sure, so I had another reason to leave at the end of the trial period.

Chapter Four

The first week of my incarceration went slowly, the best part for me was there was only one week to go then I can go back to normal life with more gratitude for the freedom I had before coming here. I also was quick to note that I had not been chastised once, although I am sure my Mistress could have easily found fault with some of my work. I worked long hours, but there was no bullying or cajoling which I had expected. I am instead just given my duties and expected to get on with them.

In many ways, I wished they had found fault with me then when the trial period is up I would have more reason to say we weren't suited. The second week began with me doing the previous week's laundry and ironing. This took pretty much all day to wash the different sorts of clothes in separate cycles, dry and iron them, then put them into different baskets, Master's, Mistress's and mine and take them to their respective bedrooms and pack the clothes away in the various cupboards.

During my afternoon tea break, I fell asleep on the kitchen chair. I was woken by my Mistress, but again, she didn't tell me off, just told me to drink my cold tea and get back to work. At the end of the day I was in no mood for sex with Master, but slaves don't have the luxury of being tired or having a headache, a slave has to perform no matter how dreadful she feels. Yes, I referred to myself as 'she' as there was no vestige of my previous male existence left to cling to. I was feeling more and more female as the days went by. On my first day, it felt strange to wear women's clothes. The cool air going up my skirt was a new sensation; the tickle of an earring against my cheek was strange. Now it all felt normal and I only remind myself I was indeed dressed as a woman when I occasionally got a glimpse of myself in one of the many mirrors around the house.

In many respects, I didn't mind being a maid. I even enjoyed being bossed around a bit and I liked feeling humbled and feeling lowly. I just wasn't at all sure I could do this on a forever basis.

I wasn't sure about my sexuality either, I didn't mind being with a man, but I wouldn't have sought my Master out, or had I found him attractive. My Master wasn't ugly and he looked after himself and was quite trim, but nevertheless, I was drawn emotionally to women and related to my Mistress better, although she wanted nothing from me sexually only hard domestic work.

Anal sex wasn't a success as such and my Master gave me a dildo to use when on my own to open me up a bit so I could take his penis more comfortably. He also threatened to put me in a butt plug all day but hadn't done anything about it as yet. Hopefully, my two weeks will be up before he gets around to it. The most humiliating thing I have done to date is scrubbing the kitchen floor on my hands and knees with both my Master and Mistress present in the room sitting at the kitchen table chatting about the bills. They took absolutely no notice of me scrubbing around them, it made me feel very lowly and insignificant.

The first day of my second week started badly as I had left the garden shed door open overnight and it was swinging on its hinges. I got told off for the first time. I wasn't punished just warned not to do it again. Yet the very next day I had done it again, I hadn't closed the garden shed door properly and at some time during the night, it came open. It made such a din my Master had to get up in the middle of the night and go and close it. Again, I got told off, but I wasn't punished. I wasn't going to chance a third time and whenever I went to the shed, I ensure the door was latched properly.

I didn't understand why I wasn't punished when I made the same bad error twice. Still, I wasn't going to tempt fate and ask why I wasn't dealt with more severely. Master and Mistress started using the wood burner as the weather was getting colder. It was still autumn, but out here in the countryside, it cooled down quite a lot at night. Now I had a new duty to clean out the wood burner as my first chore of the day. I was shown a spot in the garden where I was to empty the ash and where new wood and kindling were stored. I had to set the burner up for the next night with logs, kindling and newspaper. I also had to polish the device which was bright enamel red with brass fittings and made a lovely eye-catching addition to the living room. I had to use a special cleaner to polish the wood burner and I discovered it left a smeared residue on the glass. Again, I wasn't punished or shouted as much, just told to be more careful with my cleaning. Another duty I did at much the same time was to draw up all the blinds when the sun came up, about an hour after I started working and I had to draw them closed again at night as soon as the light went down.

On Tuesday and the second day of the second week, I did something different which broke the monotony nicely. My Master was into beekeeping and I was tasked with painting the bee hives with a special wood preserver so the hives could be stored for the winter. I was enjoying my time with the couple more as I realised I only had a few days to go then I could make my excuses and leave. I know they will likely be disappointed, but all the same, they got two weeks of work out of me for nothing, so they had gained and profited by my being here, and there was no need for me to reproach myself even though I wasn't entirely honest with them from the onset.

The last couple of days were back to the usual drudgery of cleaning, polishing and changing the beds. My Mistress was talking about me helping her in the garden when the winter is over and the weather begins to warm up. I was a little disappointed about this as they were expecting me to remain their slave after the trial period and planning for that eventuality, which meant I will have to bring an end to the trial myself and was debating about what plausible excuse I could make to say I want to leave when the trial is finished.

The last day of my trial finally arrived. Not once during the entire trial had I been chastised. I was told quite clearly from the onset I would be chastised if the standards were to slip. Chastisement was also to be used to keep me submissive, at least that was what I was told before arrived. I had a sleepless night as I dreaded telling my Master and Mistress I wanted to leave after all I couldn't fault my treatment or use it as an excuse. I thought of all sorts of excuses, but settled on being slightly more truthful and just say I didn't think things would work out long-term and they would be better off looking for someone else.

I was surprised that as the day wore on, my Mistress and Master had said nothing about our trial coming to an end, they just carried on as normal. I had been expecting them at some point in the day for my Master or Mistress to take me aside and talk about the end of the trial and where we go from here, but nothing was said at all. It was becoming more and more clear that if anything was going to be said, I shall have to instigate it not something I relished doing.

I decided to wait until the evening meal, if nothing was said by them at this time I would bring the subject up for discussion. However, nothing was said to me at all. I concluded that they were happy for me to remain as their slave and assumed I was happy to stay, therefore there was no need to bring up the fact the trial had come to an end. I waited until we had the evening meal and I had cleared away the dishes.

Chapter Five

When I had finished all my chores of the day I went into the living room where I found both Master and Mistress.

"I am glad you're here Rosie," Mistress said, "can you bring us both a cup of coffee?" I was about to speak, but thought better of it, and decided it could wait until I returned with the coffee they requested. When I returned with a tray of coffee, I asked if I could have a word. Both Master and Mistress looked at me bewildered as they could see I was anxious to speak and indicated I should sit on the sofa and say what I had come to say. I did as suggested and gingerly sat down on the edge of the sofa as I didn't want to feel or appear too comfortable.

"Yes," Mistress said, "I can see you have something on your mind, out with it."

"Today is the end of our trial period," I said nervously crocking out the words. Master and Mistress looked at each other in surprise.

"You know, neither of us had realised," Master said being the first to reply.

"Yes," Mistress added, "time has shot by so fast, that neither of us has realised that you have been with us now for two whole weeks." Mistress could see I was agitated and wanted to say more. "You're not here just to tell us the trial is over, there is something else on your mind, let's hear it?"

"As the trial has ended," I said, almost knowing their reaction in advance, "I would like to leave."

"Why?" Master intervened shocked by my revelation.

"I feel it won't work out for the long term. I don't think lifetime slavery is right for me."

"I think you have misunderstood our arrangement Rosie," Master said annoyed at me. "The arrangement was perfectly clear. You agreed to be our lifelong slave. We had written you dozens of letters where you indicated you clearly understood what you were getting yourself into.

"We went to great lengths to ensure you understood what a lifetime slave meant," Mistress added showing equal disappointment in me.

"The trial period you speak of," Master went on to say, "was for us, not you. It was for us to decide if we wanted you for a slave, you had already agreed to a life of slavery. So the answer is no, so go about your work, before I become really annoyed.

"No, no, I must leave," I demanded. "I want to go today. I added decisively."

"We are very disappointed in you Rosie," Master said. "We can't keep you here against your will."

'You may leave now by the kitchen door," Mistress said, standing and waiting for me to follow her. I will show you out." I was shocked by the instantaneousness of it all. I expected more of a discussion, a debrief if you like, I hadn't expected to be shown the door so quickly. I realised that my return rail tickets are in my wash bag. I didn't have much in the way of things, but I needed to retrieve that along with a jumper and coat.

'May I go and pack first?" I asked.

'Pack, pack," Mistress said incredulously and with some drama. "You don't own anything to pack, no, you want to leave, you leave as you came with nothing. Come with me, I'll show you out. I will allow you to keep the dress you have on, although technically that too belongs to us."

I tried to make further protests but Mistress was becoming quite animated and pushed and shoved me out of the living into the kitchen and out the back door with a loud slam shut.

I realised I hadn't in any way calculated for this response. Neither had I thought things through and considered this possible reaction by my Master and Mistress. Now I was outside in the mist and drizzle wearing only a thin frock, no cardigan, coat, money or suitable walking shoes.

I sat on the flagstone step at the kitchen door and assess and re-evaluated my predicament. I didn't know what to do so I hung fast. A short while later without any comment my Master opened the door and passed me a supermarket carrier bag. In it were my makeup and toiletry bag and a cheese sandwich wrapped in a paper bag.

At least I had my toiletry bag and I hastily looked in the lining for my railway ticket. I quickly learned a toiletry bag was no place to keep such an item. The damp had got to the ticket and as I tried to retrieve it, it turned into mush. Now my situation instead of having improved was as dire as it was when I was first thrown out the back door.

I had nowhere to go so there was no point in moving at least the wall of the house gave me some protection from the rain and wind. If I go out in the open I'll be in an even bigger mess without warm clothes and a raincoat. It also dawned on me, that I could not shave. Whilst I was passable as a girl right now, I won't be in a few hours once a beard begins to show. How could I possibly go anywhere in this sorry state, in a few short hours I'll look ridiculous.

I huddled on the doorstep to try and keep warm, I wrapped myself up as much as I could in the foetal position with my arms around my knees and shivered convulsively. I don't know how many hours I had been there shivering and getting wetter and wetter as the drizzle slowly turned into rain. I heard someone in the kitchen behind me moving around. I could also hear the conversation, but it was too low in volume for me to deduce what was being said.

Then I heard the door creak open behind me. I jumped nervously to my feet. The Master was standing there with his arms on his hips. I felt the warmth from the kitchen, sweep around me which gave me momentary relief.

"I thought I could hear movement, what are you still doing here? Why haven't you left for home?" He asked.

"I haven't any money for the train and I haven't a cardigan or coat. Neither do I know where I am exactly. Which way do I go?"

"Swaffham is in that direction," Master said, pointing with his hand, and then he turned to go back indoors.

"Can I change my mind?" I asked. "I have decided I would very much like to be your slave." My thought processes have changed completely, the thought of being inside in the warm, with three cooked meals a day seemed quite attractive now I am on the pavement with no money, coat or any way to get back home.

"You're saying that because you're out here freezing and feeling sorry for yourself. If we took you back, who is to say in a week or two you'll want to leave again? We want someone who wants to be a slave and is happy with that way of life. You should have thought of the consequences before deciding to leave us. You have made your bed, now you can lie in it." Master said, shutting the door, leaving me once again alone, cold and wet. It was also now dark and I was feeling quite sorry for myself and regretted my decision.

I huddled back up in a ball again and felt the rain drip off my hair and into my lap. Where could I go? I asked myself. I knew from the drive here we are miles away from Swaffham how long would it take to walk. No one will give me a lift as I am soaking wet. Even if I did manage to walk to Swaffham, what do I do then? I have no railway ticket now or the means to buy one.

All I could do is stay where I am and hope I can appeal to Master and Mistress's better nature and they will eventually take pity on me and at the very least let me in to warm up. However, the thoughts of such charity were diminishing as the lights were switched off as My Master and Mistress retired deeper into the house. Now I felt more alone. The rain had reverted back to drizzle, but it was getting noticeably colder as the minutes went by.

When the living room light went off and Master and Mistress retired for the night. I huddled closer to the back door to make the most of the heat from the kitchen. Remarkably, despite the cold and wet, I did manage to drift off to sleep here and there and was fast asleep when I heard the back door open. I was too sleepy to respond fast enough and I somewhat pathetically fell backwards into the kitchen.

Mistress stood there looking at the sorrowful heap on the floor. I looked up at her ankles, then her knees and then her face peering down at me as if I was something the cat had dragged in.

"What are you still doing here Rosie, you should be halfway back home now?"

"I have nowhere to go?" I replied staggering to my feet. At this point, Master heard my voice coming into the kitchen to see what was going on.

"What do you mean, you have nowhere to go?" Mistress asked in an aggressive voice.

"I have no money to go home. I would like to have another chance and be your slave again. I realise it is for life, I understand that, you won't have any more trouble with me."

"I have to do something with her, or her next trip will be to the hospital," Mistress remarked to her husband. "Go and warm yourself in front of the range. Now go on before you catch the death of cold. I don't know why I am being so charitable you don't deserve it."

Master got a kitchen chair and put it next to the range so I could sit and thaw out. The warmth of the range brought me out in uncontrollable shivers, and Mistress realised there was no point in talking to me anymore until I warmed up. Kindly she brought me a cup of tomato soup and a bread roll.

"You just sit there and warm up, when you're not at death's door, you may go and shower and change into something dry, Mistress said as she passed me my cup of soup. After twenty minutes or so and I began to feel a little more alive and I was sent upstairs to shower and change. Just as I left to go upstairs, Mistress said as I was leaving the room.

"When you have showered and changed come back down to the kitchen and we shall discuss what we are going to do with you." I nodded acknowledgement and made my way upstairs to the shower room. A shower was just what I needed to get to feel warm all over and back to my old self. It was also nice to climb into some dry clothes and put on a warm cardigan. I now felt considerably more human, but I was worried about what would happen when I get back downstairs. Would Master and Mistress take me back as their slave, or do they intend to drive me into Swaffham and leave me to my own devices? Maybe they will give me some cash to get down south, whatever their intentions, I needed to go downstairs and find out what they are going to do with me.

Chapter Six

When I stepped into the living room, both Master and Mistress were there, and each gave me a stern look before speaking. They indicated they wanted me to sit. I was about to sit in a vacant seat when Mistress barked at me, not on a seat, you may sit on the floor between us. I knelt on the rug and nervously put my hands behind my back submissively.

"We have decided whilst you were upstairs showering to give you a choice," Mistress said, pausing for me to assimilate what was said. You're very lucky in as much as your two weeks' service has been satisfactory, if it wasn't for that you would once again be shown the kitchen door."

"However, we have decided to give you two choices," Master said looking down at me. "Do you want to tell her or shall I?" Master asked his wife.

"I'll start," Mistress said. Choice One, you leave this house in the next fifteen minutes, we will pay for your taxi to Swaffham, what you do with yourself from then on is your own affair we won't want to hear from you again."

"What is Choice Two?" I asked respectfully not wishing to antagonise my Master and Mistress anymore.

"Choice Two, is you remain our slave for life," Mistress said.

"I would like to stay please?" I replied almost without any hesitation.

"Before you agree there are caveats," Master said sternly. "You'll be treated much more strictly than before."

"We have decided we were far too gentle with you up to now and that is our mistake, we believe that is where we went wrong," Mistress said. "From now on you'll be at the end of a whip until you are completely broken in, to our satisfaction. We will teach you to walk, talk and behave exactly as we want you to. You'll be punished for the smallest indiscretion, no more leniency."

'Also," Master warned, "when the two of us go out together for an afternoon or evening leaving you on your own, you'll be restrained until we return. This will only stop when we have learned to trust you again."

'Now go to the kitchen and have a good think, wait exactly ten minutes and come back in here and tell us your decision. Before you go," Mistress added. Remember this is your last chance to leave, if you stay, you won't be asked to leave again, instead, you'll be whipped until you submit. Now go and return in exactly ten minutes with your decision."

I left the room and went into the kitchen as requested. I walked up to the back door and peered out of the window, the rain had stopped, but nevertheless, it looked uninviting and very cold. Being out there with no money dressed as the opposite sex was no place to be, had I any choice at all? Nevertheless, I agonised over which way to jump. I realised both choices were final in their own way.

I looked up at the kitchen clock I still had another eight minutes to come to a decision. I debated on whether or not I could make it home from Swaffham. I could hitchhike, but dressed as a girl I would be extremely vulnerable and decided all, in all, that was a bad idea, which left one choice to be a domestic slave forever. Would it be that bad I asked myself. I would at least be in the warm, with a roof over my head and three meals a day life could be worse, or could it?

The clock ticked away and at exactly the passing of ten minutes, I stepped back into the living room. There was a momentarily eerie silence as I waited for either the Master or Mistress to speak.

"Well," Mistress barked, "Do you have something to tell us?"

"Yes," I croaked, whilst I still tossed mental coins in the air, even at this late moment I hadn't completely made up my mind, but I knew in the next split second I had to choose. "I would like to stay and be your domestic slave for life." I did it, I committed myself and was already regretting it.

"It is late now we will start afresh tomorrow," Mistress said, looking a little relieved. I don't think she fancied doing all the domestic work herself again. "First though I have something to show you. Come with me." We stepped out into the hallway and halfway along there was a sideboard, Mistress stopped and open the top drawer.

"You'll need to know where this is kept," she said opening the drawer. "I suspect I shall be asking you to come and fetch it often until you are completely broken in." With that remark, she produced a cream leather riding crop about two feet in length and about two-eighths of an inch thick at its narrowest point. Mistress for effect almost bent the crop in two and then passed it to me.

"Hold it, have a good look at it," Mistress said. I held it and looked at it as requested. "Go on swish it a couple of times," she insisted. I did as told and gave it a couple of half-hearted swishes. "For the moment it is yours alone, in future we shall share it, I get the handle and you get the stingy end." Mistress laid the implement back in the draw. "You now know where it is kept for when I send you for it," she concluded. "Now you may go to bed, no need to go to the Master's room tonight, get some sleep, you need it."

I had a restless night, but did manage to get some sleep and still hadn't gotten over the novelty of being warm. I think if I had remained outside any longer I would have got a chill or worse hypothermia. Everything seemed the same when I went downstairs for breakfast in the morning. I was as usual the only person up and awake at this hour. I sorted out a bowl of cereal as usual and made myself a cup of tea. Mistress is usually up about half an hour after me to give me my list of chores for the day.

As I was finishing off my cereal, I heard Mistress coming down the stairs. I knew it was her, for she had a heavier thud than Cy her husband who was a few pounds lighter in weight. She came into the kitchen and stood momentarily staring at me from the kitchen door.

"Stand up," she barked, "weren't you brought up to stand for a woman when she enters a room?" I jumped to my feet. "Come here she said, beckoning me over to her side.

"What are you?" she asked. I was still somewhat asleep and didn't know what she was getting at.

"I don't know what you mean?" I replied.

"Who are you? What are you and why are you here?" She asked.

"I'm your slave," I replied meekly.

"That's right, you're my slave," she replied approvingly. "From now on you'll behave as my slave. When I or Cy come into a room, you'll stand if sitting and curtsey. It doesn't have to be a full curtsey, a bob will do. It will be good for reminding you of your status. Now let's look at you." Mistress studied my makeup. "Your makeup isn't good enough, we will have paying guests soon, and I will want you to look as passable as you can be. Your makeup is sloppy and rushed. I want you in full makeup every single day. If isn't done right in the future, you'll be punished before the day has started. Put out your hands," she barked. I did so and she turned them over several times and said:

'There is dirt under your nails, in future you'll be punished for that too. Are you wearing your rubber gloves?" Before I could reply, she added. 'Make sure you do as you spend so much of your time with your hands in water, you'll get dermatitis if you don't watch it. Dermatitis is punishable too. I can't have the guests seeing you with dermatitis, so make sure you wear your gloves and cream your hands every day. Have you finished your breakfast?"

"Yes," I replied.

"Then we will begin work. "You can start with the top floor, clean every room. I will be up in an hour to see how you're getting on. A warning, anything not done properly will be punished."

I left Mistress and went upstairs to begin my chores. I carried on as normal and did the best I could. However, I came over in a cold sweat as I heard Mistress coming up the stairs probably to check on me. She ignored me at first and just went into one room after another and finally inspected the bathroom.

"Rosie, come here", she barked from the bathroom. I dropped what I was doing and ran into the bathroom. "What did I tell you this morning?" Mistress barked even louder, so loud

I shuddered. I just stood there not knowing what she meant.

"When you came into the bathroom you failed to curtsey to your Mistress.

"Sorry Mistress," I replied pathetically. "I won't forget in future."

"No you won't that is one stroke of the crop. Look she said running her finger across the window ledges, dust," She announced in disgust. "You haven't cleaned it and you also forgot the windows and the sills in the other rooms."

"Lick the windowsill clean with your tongue," Mistress demanded

"What?" I asked incredulously.

"You heard lick the dust off the windowsill, now," she bellowed. I started to lick the dust off the sill, it was so humiliating I burst into tears as

I did so. I was overwhelmed by her change in attitude towards me.

"You can stop now. The taste of dust isn't very nice is it Rosie?" Mistress asked.

" No Mistress, sorry Mistress," I replied through tears.

"You will be. Now go and clean the rest of the windowsills properly. When you have finished, go downstairs and fetch the riding crop and bring it to me in the living room. It is time for you to be acquainted with the crop properly.

I cleaned the remaining sills and when satisfied with my efforts, I left to go downstairs. When I reached the downstairs hall I went to the sideboard and fetched the riding crop for Mistress. As I carried the implement to the living room to give to Mistress I wondered what it would feel like. It was quite a stout riding crop and it was going to hurt a lot. I stepped into the living room where Mistress was relaxing and reading a magazine.

She looked up from her magazine and said:

"Good, take the crop into the kitchen and wait for me. Oh, by the way, you have earned another stroke you failed to curtsey again. Don't worry, once you have had the crop a few times you'll start to remember. Right, I'll see you in the kitchen in a minute go and wait for me there."

I stepped into the kitchen. I thought it inappropriate to sit and stood holding the crop until my Mistress arrived. I was there for what seemed like an age, it appeared my Mistress was in no hurry to deal with me. The waiting was agony I really wanted to get the punishment over and done with as I was sure the pain wouldn't be as bad as the anticipation of what was to come. I suppose I could have been there pacing up and down the kitchen for a good half an hour before my Mistress finally arrived.

I heard Mistress's familiar footsteps coming towards the door which was quite a relief the wait was now over. Without a word she beckoned for the riddling crop which I handed over to her. She then went and pulled out a chair from under the kitchen table and dragged it making a screeching sound to the centre of the room.

"Bend over the back of the chair and hold the base," Mistress demanded solemnly. I did as I was told. Mistress then lifted my skirt until it fell over my back and covered my head like a tent. Then after a second or two, she pulled down my knickers and then I felt the crop gently resting on my buttocks as if aiming.

"As this is your first punishment you'll receive six strokes, brace yourself they will hurt a lot."

With that remark, I felt the crop lift off my bottom and with a swish, it crashed down again. The pain was much more than I ever imagined, it was like being connected to the electric mains for a second.

'Count the strokes," Mistress insisted, "and say thank you after each stroke." I wriggled, cried and after the third stroke stood up and said I couldn't take anymore. The mistress was unimpressed and I was made to bend back over and receive the last three strokes.

'Right," Mistress said at the end of the punishment, "stand up and straighten your dress." I did so and was told to put the chair back under the kitchen table as it was before. 'You have got off lightly Rosie in future the minimum strokes of the riding crop will be twelve and often more depending on the misdemeanour. Now go, put the riding crop away and clean the second floor. I'll be up later to check your work." I stepped towards the kitchen door when Mistress stopped me momentarily to say. "Don't think just because you have been punished once today that I won't punish you again, if your work isn't up to stretch you'll be down here and across that chair for another cropping."

I got the impression she enjoyed punishing me and I believed her when she said she would think twice about doing it a second time in one day. My bottom throbbed profusely as I went to start cleaning the second floor. I wasn't punished again that day and I also remembered to give her a little bob each time she came into the same room as me.

The next day was laundry day and it was usual for me to spend the vast bulk of the day in the utility room doing the washing, drying and ironing. I preferred laundry day to any other day of the week as the work was less demanding and I was pretty much left to get on with the chore without interference. That was until today. I had just finished the first wash and got it dried and ironed. Whilst I was waiting for the tumble dryer to finish the second load, I sat on the floor as my back ached from the ironing I had just done. I hadn't long been on the floor when Mistress came into the utility room.

"Having a day off are we, Rosie, finding the work too much?" Mistress barked. I bounced to my feet and gave her a quick bob. "Go and get the crop and take it to the kitchen and wait for me."

Just like the day before I was waiting for an age in the kitchen for Mistress to arrive. I dreaded the outcome, even more, this time as I knew I would receive at least twelve strokes on an already much-bruised bottom.

Again, I bent over the kitchen chair and had to hold the base firmly whilst the punishment was given. There was no ceremony the twelve strokes came crashing down in quick succession and I had to thank Mistress for each. I was relieved the punishment stopped at twelve strokes, I don't think I could have taken many more without collapsing into a heap. It was barely nine o'clock in the morning and I had had my first punishment of the day.

Right straighten your clothes," Mistress said at the end of the punishment. She stepped up to me and mopped away a tear with the end of a tissue. "Being broken in isn't fun is it, Rosie, you have yet to understand who and what you are. As you're finding the work too much, you may have a day off," Mistress added with a smirk.

"Go and stand in the corner. Do not move not so much as a twitch, if I see you move you'll be back over this chair for another twelve strokes. Now go and stand in the corner." I went to the corner of the room. Mistress followed me and pushed me in tight in the corner so I could see nothing but a plain light blue wall. "Stay there until I tell you, you can come out."

I heard Mistress moving around the kitchen, she also came and left a few times. I dared not move as I never knew quite where she was. I was standing in the corner for an age. I wondered what the time may be. When I was sure Mistress was out of the room, I quickly turned to look at the clock and turned back in an instant. The time was 1:15 pm. I had been in the corner for over four hours. My legs began to ache and I was becoming desperate for a pee. I wondered how much longer I will be in the corner. A while later, both Master and Mistress came into the kitchen.

They were talking about paying guests who were shortly to arrive. After a while, Master said to me.

"What are you doing in the corner, Rosie?"

"Don't speak to her," Mistress interposed. "Rosie is under punishment, she wanted a day off so she is having one."

"Oh," Master replied, "what about the laundry?"

"Rosie can do it tomorrow along with her other chores. Now let her enjoy her day off, hopefully, she won't request another one for a while. Master and Mistress had lunch while I was still in the corner. I was getting hungry, busting for a pee and thirsty, but I dare not move. Dinner time came and went and I was still in the corner. I had been looking at a wall for ten hours. If I had a choice between standing in the corner or being whipped, I would have chosen the whip. I was actually crying with the boredom and my legs were stiff and sore. Finally, Mistress said:

'Rosie, you can come out of the corner now." I turned to face her and the Master sat at the kitchen table. "Have you enjoyed your day off?" Mistress asked, clearly seeing I was in tears. 'Perhaps that will be enough and you won't want time off for a while. You may go to the bathroom and when you return you may have your dinner, but I am afraid it is now cold.

Chapter Seven

The next day I was back in the utility room finishing off the laundry. When my back started to ache from the ironing, I would rest my back against one of the units, so if Mistress came into the room, I would be standing up and could appear to be busy, there was no way I wanted another "day off ". I had to rush my work as I had the whole of the ground floor to clean before my day would be over. Not that my day would be over even then as I would have to go to the Master's room before bed to see if he required my services.

Later that afternoon Master returned from an afternoon out with lots of packages which he took down to the cellar. When he had finished he came and found me cleaning the living room.

"You may leave this," he said, "I have another urgent job for you in the cellar. I followed Master down a short stone staircase to the cellar When I arrived, I saw several packages lying against a wall. Whilst I looked at the packages,

Master gave me a little elementary toolbox. "You can unwrap it all and assemble it, come and find me when you have finished."

Master hadn't said what it is so I was quite intrigued by what was hidden under the wrappings. I eagerly tore off the paper and it quickly became clear what it was I was about to make. It was a large cage that might be used to keep a big dog in, but I guessed it wasn't for a dog as Master and Mistress only had a white fluffy cat.

I set about putting the cage together. It didn't take too long it was basically a big rectangle with a hinged door. There was also an inch-thick padded mat to go on the floor. When I finished putting the cage together to my satisfaction, I went to find Master to tell him the job was done. The master seemed pleased when I told him I had finished building the cage.

"Rosie has built the cage, do you want to come downstairs and see it? He asked his wife.

"Yes, Mistress replied excitedly, "I am keen to see what it looks like."

"You can come too Rosie," Master said.

I followed the Master and Mistress down to the cellar. I stepped in behind them as they admired my workmanship.

"That will be perfect," Mistress said approvingly.

"Yes, that is what I thought," replied the Master. "I presume you know what this is for?" Master asked, turning to look at me. I knew exactly what it was for but I didn't let on and shook my head.

"Do you remember the conversation we had the day before yesterday after you decided to renew your commitment to be our slave?"

"Yes Master," I replied.

"Then you remember the part about you being restrained on the occasions when both Mistress and I go out."

"This is for you Rosie, would you like to step in and try it out for size," Mistress said opening the door for me. I stepped in. I had to bend my head forward as there was not the height to stand up straight, but at least it had a padded mat and if I lie down I would almost be able to stretch my legs out. I suppose I should be grateful as the Master could have bought a smaller cage which would be even less comfortable.

"You get to try it out tonight," Mistress said with a satisfied smile. "We are off to a concert in Swaffham and won't be back until quite late."

"The cage is to ensure you'll still be here safe and sound on our return. We don't want you to be tempted to leave again. Our guest arrives in a couple of days and we need a domestic servant."

After dinner, I was taken back down to the cellar and put in the cage. The master put a padlock on the cage door and locked me in. He also passed me a bottle in case I need a pee while they were out. The master went on to say:

"Originally we were just going to tie you in a chair in the kitchen when we're out, but we will have guests by Friday, so you needed to be somewhere where the guests won't go. We are also going to put some chains and things on the wall, as in the future, you'll also need to come down here to be punished as it is quite soundproof down here and again out of bounds to our guests. Well, as there is nothing for you to do, you won't need the light on, I'll switch it off as I go."

With that Master left, leaving me locked in my cage and I was plunged into total darkness as he extinguished the light as he left. All I had was a small sliver of light from under the cellar door. I was left that way until the morning when my Master came down to the cellar to unlock me from my cage.

'When you have had your breakfast," he said. 'Collect your things from your bedroom and bring them down here to the cellar."

'Why?" I asked.

'Why? Why? You don't ask why you're a slave you just do as you're told unless you would like to fetch the whip first." Master replied with a burst of anger. Then in an instant, he calmed down a bit and added:

'If you must know we have decided you can sleep in the cellar and free up your room for rent to the public. You can sleep in your cage, but don't worry, you'll only be locked in when Mistress and I go out for the day or an evening. Also in the future, you'll be sent to the cellar for chastisement, as we don't want to alarm the guests."

When I had finished breakfast and had brought my things down to the cellar, my first job of the day was as a chambermaid and I had to change all the bed linen on all beds in the house which mounted to six beds including Master and Mistress's beds. I hadn't realised just how much hard work it is to change one bed after another. I felt sorry for hotel chambermaids who would have to change beds all day long and do nothing else. After six-bed changes, I was exhausted. It wasn't just the physical changing of the sheets, etc. it was also I had to bring up fresh linen and take downstairs soiled bed linen two, or three flights of stairs to be washed. I also had to clean the rooms as well which were inspected by my Mistress a short while later.

By the time I got to the Master's bedroom in the evening, I was at a point of total exhaustion. I would try to arouse Master as quickly as I could so he would cum in the shortest time possible once he had ejaculated I would be dismissed and could go to bed.

Except, I no longer had a bed to go to, just the floor of the cage with a thin foam rubber mat for me to lie on, the only saving grace was I had one less bed to change. Although the rubber mat felt soft and comfortable for an hour or so it soon felt no softer than the concrete floor. All I had was a blanket to cover myself with, neither could I lie down straight and had to lie at an angle to stretch my legs fully. However, I am too tired tonight for these discomforts to bother me and I soon fell asleep.

I woke in the morning abruptly and was startled by the riding crop crashing down on my back and buttocks. "Come out of the cage so I can punish you properly," Mistress said as she continued to whip me as I desperately tried to shield my body from the blows. I cried, struggled and pleaded with her to stop. Mistress stopped lashing at me to say:

"You have overslept. Now get out of the cage." I crawled out of the cage and stood before Mistress. "What are you?" Mistress asked. This question was getting a little tedious, but I replied:

"I am your slave Mistress."

"Yes, you're my slave and my slaves do not oversleep, now go and bring your chair to the middle of the room and bend over the back, and we will continue to punish you in a civilised manner." I bent over the chair and Mistress lifted my nightie over my head and resumed beating me with the riding crop. God only knows how many strokes I had of the riding crop when Mistress finished, it was way over the statuary twelve and I was crying, stinging mass of humanity when Mistress finally stopped wielding the riding crop on my behind.

"Stand up," she shouted and put the chair back against the wall and return and stand at my feet. I did as I was told to put the chair back and stood about two feet from her. Mistress pulled a tissue from the sleeve of her dress and began to mop my tears, which made me feel very sorry for myself and I cried even more. "I don't think you quite understand what being a slave is all about yet do you Rosie? You are the lowest thing on this earth you have no value at all. You also have no rights, not one except to work hard. You're the lowest of the low and only good for very menial work, in other words, a skivvy.

You're no longer a free person Rosie, we own you," she stopped for effect and continued to exaggeratedly wipe away my tears with a cynical "there, there," for effect.

"If I want to beat you until you bleed, I shall beat you until you bleed," Mistress assured me. "You have no rights, none whatsoever, the sooner you learn that the better for you. You're a long way from being broken in, but we will, mark my words, break you in. Eventually, you'll be a perfectly submissive, servile, passive and compliant slave, even you will be proud of yourself."

" Are you going to sleep in again, Rosie?" Mistress asked.

"No Mistress," I replied

"You can forgo breakfast and go about your duties, I'll be along to check your work later."

Chapter Eight

t became a daily campaign for my Mistress and Master to make me feel completely worthless and without any value. The work I provided was considered more trouble than I was worth as I had to be under constant chastisement and supervision. Life was a succession of drudgery without any breaks or respite. At least twice a week I was taken to the cellar and locked in my cage. If this occurred during the working day I would have to make up any chores I had missed the next day even if it took well into the night.

My treatment had a psychological effect as I was beginning to accept I was as worthless as my owners would have me believe. Although this couldn't possibly be true as I did all the housework every last bit of it, if I was suddenly to leave, they would without a doubt notice I had gone. I was in reality saving my Master a fortune in wages when you considered on an average day I worked 12 to 14 hours. Just like everything else in life, humans adapt and I was getting used to what I had and making the most of my situation. Nevertheless, no matter how hard I tried to please it was never good enough for my Mistress. Every day she would inspect my work with a fine-toothed comb and the smallest error was dealt with chastisement.

Paying guests had started to arrive now and my workload doubled. I was told not to talk to guests, but if they spoke to me I was to give short replies, not engage in conversation and go about my business. One evening when my work was done, I was called into the living room which was a rare event, normally when the work was done, I had to stop in the kitchen if I wanted to sit awhile or make a drink. This evening, though Mistress came into the kitchen and told me she wanted to chat and I was to go into the living room.

I followed Mistress back into the living room and was allowed to sit on the rug between Mistress and Master. Mistress began the conversation:

"We hadn't really bothered much until now because there had only been the three of us. However, now we have guests, we have noticed that although at a glance you look convincingly female, however, on closer observation there is a lot that gives you away as a male. We feel you should have some female deportment training in the evenings. Anything to say before we continue?" Mistress asked.

"I don't understand?" I replied.

"In a nutshell, we want you to behave and act more femininely, it is that hard to understand, is it?" Mistress bellowed. "We have already had comments about you and we have only had guests for the last two days. We feel with some intensive training you'll pass as a female more effectively. Now, do you understand?"

"Yes, Mistress, I am sorry I am not girlish enough."

"You will be Rosie, we shall see to that," Master said, speaking for the first time since I entered the room.

"Every evening you will come into the living room with us and we will give you deportment lessons, which will continue until we are satisfied that you walk, talk and act like a female. No time like the present, we shall start tonight. I have taken the trouble to fetch the riding crop in advance in case you need some extra encouragement."

"We are aiming for a total transformation in your behaviour after a couple of weeks of intensive training. Master added.

"No time like the present we will start now," Mistress said. "Go and walk to the door and back." I did as Mistress asked and sauntered over to the door, turned on my heels and walked back."

"No, no that is not how a lady walks. Correction, my apologies, you're not and will never be a lady, you're a servant girl. Women do not walk with their arms out like an ape, that's how men walk. Watch me," she said. Mistress walked to the living room door and back.

"Tell me, Rosie, what was the difference between my walk and yours?" Mistress asked as she held the riding crop in both hands flexing it very slightly. I could hear the leather squeak as she did so.

"Um, you had your arms close to your side," I replied, hoping that was the right answer.

"Yes, clever girl, now you try," Mistress said pointing to the door. I did so and was told to repeat the walk several times to get used to keeping my arms down at my sides and undo years of walking like an ape.

"Now, Rosie, I want you to continue walking to the door, this time taking much shorter steps, women don't stride as men do, they walk in neat little steps, now you try."

"No, no, no," Mistress bellowed, you're still striding. Come here. Bend over the back of the sofa. I was almost pushed into position. Then Mistress unceremoniously lifted my skirt and roughly pulled down my panties. "You're still bruised from when I punished you last, a pity as you'll have new bruises now," she said giving me three hard smacks of the crop. "You'll need to learn quickly or you're going to have a very sore bottom over the next couple of weeks. Now try again, short feminine little steps."

I walk up and down to the door several times before Mistress was satisfied. Luckily Master was getting thirsty, so I was dismissed from deportment lessons to go and make coffee. The next evening was lessons on how to stand and sit. I was told I won't be doing much in the way of sitting, but nevertheless, I needed to know how to sit in a feminine fashion.

I had to bring into the living room a hard-packed chair from the kitchen for these exercises. I was told to always smooth my skirt before I sat down and to keep my legs together at all times. I was taught the Duchess of York pose and to cross my legs at the ankles and not at the knee. All this extra instruction was interspersed with liberal use of the crop, in particular the little flap at the end.

The hardest part of my female deportment was yet to come, and that comprised of speech lessons to make my voice more feminine by raising the pitch of my voice by a notch or two to sound more feminine. My voice was naturally low, but I was beaten black and blue until my voice sounded much more feminine. It took so much effort to change my voice, I eventually found it hard to revert to my old voice even if I wanted to. I also had to take more care of my makeup and Mistress would examine me every morning, and god help me if I was sent back to the cellar to redo my makeup

Mistress had decided I was getting hardened to the riding crop and had one afternoon whilst she was out bought an eighteen-inch, thick, almost solid cow's leather tawse and she was itching for an excuse to try it out on me. When I eventually had that pleasure, the pain from the tawse was unbearable after just three strokes and I would be begging and pleading with Mistress to stop. From that moment on I feared the tawse and did what I could to avoid its further acquaintance.

Master and Mistress agreed I had finally been broken in as their slave and was reduced to a completely compliant and servile servant. They had put much of this transformation down to my genuine fear of the leather tawse which I was allowed to keep in the cellar on a hook on the wall, so I could look at it often as an incentive to be obedient.

A recession was biting hard and paying guests were beginning to dwindle as the summer went on. Not that the lack of paying guests made that much difference to my workload as the house still needed cleaning regularly from top to bottom. On top of all my domestic duties, I still needed to attend to my Master's sexual needs, which I did almost every evening. He seemed to have an insatiable appetite for sex and I appeared to be his only outlet, as I was fairly sure Mistress had long withdrawn nuptial services to her husband and I was there to take up the slack.

I remember once when washing up in the kitchen Mistress was having one of her more chatty moments and she let slip how she hated giving oral to her husband, which she reviewed as sordid, filthy and degrading, and was so pleased he now had me to provide that particular need. Like clockwork, we would alternate between one evening of oral sex and the next anal sex. I preferred anal sex as it required less effort on my part at the end of the day when I was already exhausted from housework. Sometimes after sex Master would have a little chat before I was sent off to bed for the night. He often said how much he enjoyed our sessions.

"That was nice," Master crooned after I had completed oral on his and had swallowed his seed. "Of course," he added, "Not only will you have sex with me, but you'll also have sex with anyone I tell you to. You understand that, don't you Rosie?"

"Yes Master," I replied, not giving what he had said a great deal of thought, well not at the time, but after I returned to the cellar it did play on my mind a bit, as Master hadn't said such a thing before. I did know it was customary for slaves to be offered to friends for sex by their Masters. However, in our particular case, we rarely had non-paying guests. Master and Mistress didn't seem to have much in the way of friends if any. However, it soon became clear why the Master had brought this to my attention.

All the paying guests had gone and despite two months left of the season, there were no new bookings. I often whilst performing housework overheard bits of conversation between Master and Mistress. I could tell from what they said they were getting very worried about their finances. Not only were there no guests the sales of bespoke furniture they made in the workshop had fallen off as well. Both could be considered luxuries in hard times and it is luxury items that go first. Master and Mistress were racking their brains to find new ways of bringing in much-needed revenue.

Chapter Nine

I was soon to discover what one of the new methods of revenue was to be. One afternoon whilst busying myself with housework on the top floor. I heard from the stairwell Mistress shout for me.

'Rosie, can you come down to the living room please." I stopped what I was doing and made my way downstairs. I knocked on the living room door which was closed and I was told to enter. Instead of seeing just Master and Mistress here, there was also another man sitting on the sofa. I hated curtseying with strangers around, but I bit my lip and gave a respectful dip which seemed to go down well.

'Come into the centre of the room," Mistress demanded with a funny smirk on her face. "Now do a twirl for us." It was such an odd request I did nothing for a moment. "Come on Rosie a twirl, just go around on your toes a couple of times." I reluctantly did so then Mistress added. "Right you may sit for a moment." Then the threesome continued the conversation they were having before I entered the room. Some minutes later when the male guest had finished his drink of brandy Mistress asked him.

"Well, what do you think Roger? Will Rosie do?"

"Oh yes, the man replied, Rosie looks very nice she will do nicely.

"Rosie," Mistress said, "take Roger and show him around guestroom number one." I went to the living room door waiting for Roger to follow me. As the man stood Mistress said to him. "Don't worry about the time you and Rosie go, get to know each other and enjoy yourselves."

I don't know if I was being naïve or what but it was only just dawning on me what was happening, I had been sold for sex. What was worse, I was the last person to know what was happening to me. This is the point I really felt like a slave, my body was no longer my own to the point it could be sold and bartered without me even knowing about it. I truly had become the lowest of all creatures.

I took Roger into the guest room where he produced this enormous cock and I was made to perform oral services. When it was all over he chatted for a bit and finally I showed him back to the living room. When I returned to the living room with the man, I was immediately dismissed to go and get on with my chores.

That was the end of the episode except for a couple of days later whilst washing up the dinner plates in the kitchen Mistress came over and tapped me on the shoulder.

"Do you remember Roger, who you entertained a few days ago?"

"Yes Mistress," I replied, wondering why she should mention him.

"Well, he was very pleased with you. So much so, he had booked a regular session with you every Tuesday afternoon."

"Oh," I replied with a definite lack of enthusiasm.

"It would seem you're not quite so completely useless after all. You'll also be delighted to hear you have another visitor due any time now," Mistress said looking at her watch. "So when you have done the washing up go and touch up your makeup and put on some perfume, you're becoming quite popular."

After a month or so I had four to five regular visitors plus a few one-offs. All monies are paid directly to my Master or Mistress. Needless to say, I never saw any money or was aware of how much men paid for my services.

The only good thing to be said about the whole sordid business was my body was staving off financial ruin for my owners. I brought in enough cash to help to keep them afloat. What my Master and Mistress didn't know was I occasionally got paid separately as a tip. With this money, I would squirrel away and hide under a rug in the cellar. Once I got a few hundred saved I could think about escaping again. In the meantime, though, I had to bide my time and save what money I could for as long as I could.

When I was cleaning the rooms I would also find coins on the carpet or sometimes down the side of the seats. I would keep these too, although the coins were harder to hide than banknotes, especially once they started to mount up. I would also ask clients to change coins for banknotes when I had enough which help prevent me from accumulating too many coins.

I asked if I could move into the guest room one as there were no guests and it was a room I would use to entertain Master and Mistress's "friends". However, my request was refused and was told I should be grateful I had a cage in the cellar and many slaves would sleep without a pillow on the kitchen floor each night and have no room to retreat to. Often when I retired to the cellar at night I would sit in my cage and masturbate as there wasn't much else for me to do apart from sleep.

I was masturbating one evening when Mistress came into the cellar to lock me in my cage as they decided, off the cuff, to out for the evening. Mistress caught me in the act and it was too late for me to cover myself, besides, I was also somewhat flushed and that would have been difficult to hide.

"What are you doing?" Mistress asked, sounding quite surprised as if masturbating wasn't something she expected me to do. "I can't have this," she said, "you need to save your energies for work, not self-indulgence. "Stay there I will be back shortly," she added leaving the cellar. A short while later Mistress returned with a set of handcuffs. Mistress got me to kneel up and cuffed my hands to the top of the cage. "This will do for tonight and I'll find some more permanent form of chastity for you tomorrow. It's no wonder you look so tired sometimes if you're working all day and masturbating at night as well. You're our property," Mistress assured me. "You're here to serve us, not here for your own pleasures, will soon put a stop to that."

I had to stay on my knees all night with my arms in the air. I got no sleep at all and ached all over my body. The next morning couldn't come fast enough. I was allowed out of my cage and my handcuffs were removed. No more was said, but later that afternoon I was summoned to the living room to see my Master and Mistress.

"We have something for you," Mistress said with a self-satisfied grin. "We had been shopping today and we have a present for you. Never let it be said we don't think about you when we are out."

"Thank you," I replied, not knowing what else I was supposed to say. I had yet to find out what my present was, but I knew instinctively it wouldn't be anything to get excited about.

"It's that little box on the coffee table, would you like to open it and see what it is?"

"Yes Mistress," I replied.

"Well, go on then, pick it up and open it," Master urged. I picked up the little box which was quite heavy for its size. The box was plain white cardboard, so that didn't give anything away. I gave it a customary shake which didn't tell me very much. I did note it was quite heavy for such a tiny box.

"It's not a birthday present, not that slaves have birthdays, just do as you told and open it," Mistress said somewhat frustrated with me. I took the lid off the box and pulled out a little metal cage.

"Yes," Mistress exclaimed, "it's a chastity device just for you. I'll have you know it wasn't cheap either, so we need to get our money's worth. I shall put it on for you now. Stand here in front of me. Pull down your knickers and hold your skirt up around your waist." Mistress demanded. I did as I was told. I couldn't see what was going on, my skirt was in the way. I felt the cold metal of the device and Mistress pulling and tugging at my private parts. After a few moments, Mistress exclaimed:

"That's it, that will stop you from playing with yourself. Your energy levels are for our use not for your own pleasures. Now straighten your clothes have a walk up and down the room and tell me how it feels." I did as I was told.

"It feels strange, heavy and it pinches a bit," I replied, clearly unhappy with my unwanted gift.

"You'll get used to it, you shall wear it always except when you have clients to attend to. No slave of mine is allowed to masturbate, no go away and get on with your duties."

Chapter Ten

As the months went by I assumed my slavery was complete as I felt I was reduced to the lowest denominator. I thought I had suffered every humiliation there was used, abused, worked 15 hours a day and suffered the indignation of being hired out to strangers for their sexual use. I also turned my back on my birth gender and now thought of myself as a woman and rarely thought of myself as ever having been a man.

I found it impossible to think that I could be degraded more. I was the lowest of all human beings, but there was more to come. I was now no longer allowed to address myself as 'I' or 'me' instead I had to address myself as 'Master's or Mistress's slave'. If I forgot to do this it resulted in instant punishment, usually a whipping. When there were no guests I had to wear a heavy stainless steel collar and wrist cuffs. These were removed if I was 'entertaining' or we had paid guests to come and stay with us.

I was no longer invited into the living room to watch television or relax. Instead, I had to sit in the kitchen where I could hear either my Master or Mistress call if they needed anything. I noticed my food was different to my Master's too, and I was now being fed left over's and anything that was past its best or sell-by date. Sometimes I had hardly anything to eat. If I complained I would have what little there was taken away and given a flogging instead.

I was lucky I was much the same size as Mistress or I suspect I would barely have any clothes on my back everything I wore was Mistress's at one time or another. Not that I liked wearing Mistress's old clothes as they were generally very frumpy. I knew I couldn't continue as I was, It was beginning to give me mental health issues as I slipped deeper and deeper into depression. Everything seemed so hopeless there was nothing at all to look forward to except never-ending drudgery.

I had been saving for quite a few months now and I had about one thousand pounds in cash, enough to escape and keep me going for a week or two. The problem I had is, that Master and Mistress never, ever let me out of their sight and whenever they went out I was locked up in my cage. The house was very remote with no immediate neighbours, If there was any work for me to do in the garden, I would be locked in ankle chains making it impossible for me to run off. My Master and Mistress were not going to give me the slightest opportunity to run away, I was too much of an asset for them to risk losing.

I guessed they were aware if I got half the chance I would run away even though I had promised to stay.

It was a matter of bidding my time, which wasn't easy as my life became more micromanaged as time went on. I was buoyed by the fact I had some money flittered away. However, I had to keep moving it so it would be found by either my Master or Mistress. Its discovery would not only dash any plans I may have but I would also be severely punished as they will assume I had stolen the money from them as there was on the face of it no other logical way for me to have possession of it.

My worst nightmare came true. Or to be more accurate half the worst nightmare came true. I stashed my money away in two bundles, cash and coins. My cellar had a small window which overlooked a brick wall, but it did allow precious light to enter the room. On the window was a curtain held up by a curtain rod. I discovered when removing one of the ornate ends, that the rod was hollow and it was here I hid my banknotes instead of under the rug as I had previously done. It was a perfect hiding place, who would think of looking there for anything?

Coins were harder to hide and I placed them out individually in the cellar under the hessian rug. This worked rather well as one couldn't feel the coins underfoot and I was the only one likely to ever move the mat. What I hadn't taken into account was Mistress coming down to the cellar unannounced. For a while, I had a bit of an ear infection and was a bit deaf and on this occasion, I hadn't heard Mistress coming down the stone cellar steps. At the time I was on my knees with the rug up at one of the corners so I could count and add new coins I found around the house. I only heard my Mistress approach as she got to the cellar door. I quickly put the rug back down, but there was a puff of dust and I was still on my knees which looked very suspicious.

"I have just come down to…" Mistress stopped speaking when she saw me on my knees. "What are you up to?" she asked, changing her course of conversation. "Why are you on your knees looking extremely guilty?" I climbed to my feet and stood and faced Mistress and replied:

"I was exercising," I said unconvincingly.

"I don't believe that for one moment. You have been working hard all day, why should you want to exercise, it makes no sense," Mistress replied, placing her hands on her hips to display her dominance over me. "Come on, I am not leaving until I get a proper explanation."

"I was doing press-ups," I replied, feeling myself glowing red in the face, which gave away graphically I was lying through my teeth.

"No, you weren't," Mistress said dismissively. "I am not leaving here until I get a satisfactory explanation. Now come on tell me what you were doing and quickly I don't have all evening." I rather embarrassingly stood there and said nothing; I had run out of plausible excuses. Mistress mused over my silence and I could see her temper rising.

"Now what could you be doing down on your knees?" she asked herself as she bends down towards the floor. "Could you be hiding something under the mat, is that it Rosie? Do you wish to say anything?" She asked, holding the corner of the rug. She could see on my face I had something to hide and she was going to milk my discomfort for all it was worth.

"Let's see," she said, pulling the rug back. She revealed several coins and kept pulling the rug back until they were all exposed. "What is this?" she asked, "do you want to explain why you have money under the rug? How much is there?"

"I don't know how much there is," I replied.

"Cy," Mistress shouted back up the stairs. "Can you come down here and bring with you a small shopping bag and my tawse."

"Get it all out and put the money on the table and count it, let's see how much you have."

While we were waiting for the Master to arrive I picked up all the coins and put them on a little table I had in the cellar and began to make piles of £1.00. When I had finished Mistress counted up the piles.

'Sixteen Pounds," she said at the end of the count. "How did you get this money, you have stolen it from us, haven't you?"

'It is just money I found on the floor or down the side of the seats," I replied.

'That is still stealing, it isn't your money, and you have no money of your own as you're a slave." Master arrived with a small plastic shopping bag.

'What is this?" he asked, surprised to see all the coins on the little table.

'Money Rosie has stolen from us," Mistress replied. "There is sixteen Pounds worth of silver and copper coins. "Right, Rosie put all the money in the plastic bag and take it upstairs to the living room and wait for us. While you are waiting we shall decide on your punishment.

I did as I was told and left Master and Mistress in the cellar and went upstairs to the living room. I stepped in and placed the bag of coins on the coffee table and waited for the Master and Mistress to follow. I was so pleased it was just the coins they found and not the banknotes, as I had over one thousand Pounds now and that was enough for me to risk escaping when the time was right.

The Master and Mistress returned to the living room as they entered I went down on my knees and began to beg their forgiveness.

"Don't speak," Mistress barked. "From now on you'll only speak when we address you. Then Mistress went into a tirade of abuse calling me a snivelling worthless little thief who deserves what is coming to her. While I was being verbally debased, my Master had left the room and returned with a camcorder, tripod and lighting.

I was told to go and stand against the wall whilst everything was being set up. I was told my punishment will be filmed and sold online. Mistress joked about how famous I'll become. Whilst I was standing in the corner, I was told to undress to my bra and panties. When I was undressed Mistress came over with a large white cardboard sheet with the word 'Thief' on it and placed it around my neck with a piece of string. My Mistress asked her husband if he was ready and he replied yes. Then I was ordered out of the corner.

I was pushed to the centre of the room. I hadn't noticed before, but on a beam above was a metal eye and rope had been fed through it and looped through the cuffs on my wrist. Then I was hauled up on tiptoe.

"Thieves are severely punished and I am going to whip you until you feel the warm blood drip from your back and buttocks. However," Mistress said first Master and I are going to have a cup of tea, so we shall be back to you shortly. I shall leave you this to look at." Mistress left a black leather tawse on the table so I could see it. "Back shortly," was Mistress's last remark before she and her husband left the room for the kitchen.

I was left there dangling from the ceiling on tiptoes. It only took a few short minutes for my body to begin to ache from tip to toe. The room was deadly quiet, I couldn't hear Master and Mistress in the kitchen next door, it was as if I was in the house on my own. It wasn't long before I was begging for Mistress's return. I was positively welcoming a hard beating so I could be released, my body could take much more of the stretching soon I would be crying out in pain without the tawse having touched me.

I seemed to be hanging there an hour or perhaps two waiting for my punishment to begin. I couldn't believe how relieved I was when I heard Master and Mistress's voices approach the living room door.

"I hope we haven't kept you too long," Mistress asked sarcastically.

"I'll make the camera ready, and then you can begin," Master said as I heard him fiddle with things behind me and a bright light engulfed me. In the meantime, Mistress picked up the tawse and flicked it up and down a few times in front of me for effect. It worked, although I longed to be released from my bonds, I was now dreading the tawse as well.

"I'm now ready to start filming," my Master said to his wife.

"Good," she replied, and then I'll begin.

"Cameras roll". The Master said rather dramatically. Mistress stepped behind me and I heard a final practice run of the tawse whisking through the air making a whooping sound.

"This is what happens to thieves," Mistress announced as the whip crashed on my back for the first stroke. I span on my tiptoes with the pain, but before the first lot of stinging subsided down came the second stroke. Then it was a blur of tawse strokes, pain, crying and wriggling. It only stopped when I felt warm blood trickle from my right buttock down my leg.

"Shall I switch the camera off?" Master asked.

"Yes," Mistress replied, I think she has had enough. I am hungry now let's go and have some supper."

Once again I was left on my own spinning on the rope in pain in the dark as Mistress had switched the lounge light off as she left. The pain slowly subsided to a dull thud from tip to toe. It must have been two, or three o'clock in the morning before I was released from my bonds. I fell into a heap on the floor where I had been strung up. Mistress kicked me and said.

'Drag your carcase into the kitchen and sleep on the floor we're not done with you yet. I am off to bed," she said as I crawled towards the kitchen.

Chapter Eleven

I couldn't sleep on the kitchen floor not without a pillow to rest my head. For that reason I was up early and went down to the cellar, shaved and put on fresh makeup and clothes. I wore a black frock as I was still bleeding in places.

Then I returned to the kitchen and I got myself a bowl to pour in some cereal when Mistress arrived. She was deliberately early and holding a riding crop.

"How is the thief this morning?" she asked. "You can put that bowl away, thieves don't get breakfast."

"But I haven't eaten since yesterday evening," I pleaded.

"You don't expect me to be sorry for you, do you? You're being punished.

"But if I don't eat I'll faint," I said, trying to appeal to Mistress's better nature, assuming she has one.

"Oh, you poor thing," Mistress replied sarcastically with an exaggerated look of concern. "We can't have that, can we? I can't have it said we can't look after our slave properly, even though she is a worthless thief. Let's see what we can find for you," Mistress said, walking around the kitchen with her fingers flicking her lips in concentration. "Oh yes, I have something for you," she said, gliding over to going the waste bin. She took the lid off and found scraps of pizza from the supper they had the night before. The food was covered in bits of tea leaves and other muck. She threw the glutinous, sticky mess on the floor.

"On your knees and start eating, I can't have you falling ill for lack of food."

"It's spoilt," I pleaded, "I can't eat that."

"You will," Mistress said, you'll eat every last scrap on your knees with just your mouth. I shall sit and watch you," she added pulling up a kitchen chair to watch the spectacle. I went down on my knees and looked at the inedible gloop. "Eat it, you're not getting anything else today."

I was between a rock and a hard place, either I humiliated myself or I starved. As I was already starving, I didn't have much choice. So I went on all fours and started to eat.

"That's it," Mistress said, watching me reach as I begin to eat. "There's a good girl and you will eat every last drop before you start work." With the occasional flick of the riding crop and kick on my already sore buttocks, I ate every last speck of food. Mistress amused herself as I made reaching and vomiting noises as I did so.

"Now you can wash the floor and go about your duties," Mistress said standing to leave the room. That seemed to be the end of my punishment except Mistress kept true to her word and I wasn't fed again that day. My treatment was progressively getting worse and I had to do something to get away and return to a normal life. It was coming up to my second anniversary and I was determined to get away before the due date.

One morning I went upstairs from the cellar for breakfast. At around 6:30 there is usually some commotion when the Master and Mistress stir from their slumber. Today, however, it was unusually quiet. Seven o'clock came and went and there was still no sound of my owners getting up. Then I heard a weak cry from the stairs and it was Mistress's voice:

"Rosie," come up here we need you. This was different I had never been asked to go up to their rooms in the morning they always came downstairs to me in the kitchen. Curious to know what was wrong, I went upstairs to Mistress's bedroom. I found Master and Mistress in bed together, although he had his own room. I could see straight away, they were ill and looked ashen and grey. Mistress wearily sat herself up in bed and said to me looking very weak and ill:

"We are both ill, you can drop all your normal chores and will look after us until we feel better. "Now," she said, pausing. "I want you to go to the kitchen and bring us up some cold orange juice and some aspirin. That will do for the moment, go on and go," she added, waving me away downstairs. It was a good job they had an ensuite bedroom as they took regular turns to go and vomit, clearly they were both very unwell. However, I seemed to be unaffected, although I quite expected to fall ill at any moment, especially as I was making regular visits to their infected bedroom.

I spent the morning going up and down the stairs like a Yo-Yo, at the whim of Master and

Mistress's beck and call. Whilst I was downstairs in the kitchen washing up the breakfast bowls which they had mostly left, it occurred to me I was missing a golden opportunity to escape. Master and Mistress were too ill to stop me.

At this revelation, I stopped washing the dishes and ran down to the cellar, touched up my makeup, changed my clothes to something suitable to wear outside of the house and got my money from the curtain rail. Then I went upstairs and emptied one of Mistress's handbags and put my stuff in it. I also found some more cash in the living room and added it to mine. Then I hunted for Master's car keys, fortunately, they were in the living room too. I heard a frantic shout from upstairs:

'Where are you Rosie, we need more orange juice and bring up some ice while you are at it."

I did as they asked and took up to their bedroom a tray of orange juice and a bowl of ice cubes. I entered the room and both Master and Mistress looked at me incredulously. Despite being poorly, Mistress sat bolt upright in bed and asked:

"Why have you changed your clothes and what are you doing with my handbag?"

"I am borrowing it," I replied.

"Borrowing it, borrowing it, what do you mean?" Mistress said with concern in her voice.

"I am using it to go away," I replied, deliberately being vague.

"Going away," Mistress repeated.

"Yes, I am leaving you.

"Let her go, it is only a handbag, we'll get by without her," Master said going back under the covers too ill to care about me or what I was about to do.

"That's the attitude," I replied to Master's remark, "because I am borrowing your car as well." Now Master too was sitting bolt upright looking very concerned.

"Not my car, please, it is brand new, I only got it the day before yesterday." He pleaded.

"I suspect I have mostly paid for it with all the free labour you have gotten from me. Not to mention guests who have paid for my services. I promise not to look after your car too well and you'll find it somewhere on the South Coast when I'm finished with it. I'll drop you a line to tell you where I left it."

With that remark, I haughtily turned around and minced out of the room, slamming the door behind me. I could hear both Master and Mistress clambering out of the bed, so I ran down the stairs to be ahead of them and straight outside into the car and away.

The End

Check out my other books:

The Chronicles of a Male Slave.

A real-life account of a consensual slave. The book follows the life of an individual who comes to terms with his submissive side and his search for a Mistress and his subsequent experiences as a consensual slave.

This book gives a real insight into the B.D.S.M., lifestyle and what it is like to be a real slave to a lifestyle Mistress.

Mistress Margaret.

This is the story of young teenage Brenden, who is finding out about his sexuality when he meets older Mistress Margaret a nonprofessional dominatrix. Mistress Margaret takes Brenden's hand and shows him the mysterious, erotic world of BDSM and all it has to offer.

The Week That Changed My Life.

A tale about a young girl discovering her sexuality with an older, more mature dominant man whilst on a week's holiday by the sea. She was introduced into a world of BDSM that would change her outlook on life forever.

The Temple of Gor.

Hidden in the wilds of Scotland is The Temple of Gor, a secret BDSM society. In the Temple, you will find Masters and their female slaves living in a shared commune. The community is based on the Gorean subculture depicted in a fictional novel by John Norman and has taken a step too far and turned into a macabre reality. Stella a young girl from England, stumbles on the commune and is captured and turned into a

Kajira slave girl until she finds a way to escape her captors.

Becoming a Sissy Maid.

This is a true story of one person's quest to become a sissy maid for a dominant couple. The story outlines the correspondence between the Master, Mistress, and sissy maid, that leads up to their first and second real-time meeting.

It is a fascinating tale and is a true, honest and accurate account, only the names and places have been changed to protect the individuals involved. It is a must-be-read book by anyone into BDSM and will give an interesting insight for anyone wishing to become in the future a real-time sissy maid.

Meet Maisy The Sissy Maid.

This story is about Maisy a sissy maid and her life. The story takes Maisy through all the various stages a sissy has to make take to find her true submissive and feminine self. It is a long and arduous road and many transitions before Maisy finds true happiness as a lady's maid for her Mistress.

Beginner's Guide For The Serious Sissy

So you want to be a woman and dress and behave like a sissy? You accept you cannot compete with most men and now want to try something new and different. This guide will help you along the way and walk the potential sissy through the advantages and pitfalls of living as a submissive woman.

Becoming a serious sissy requires making changes that are both physical and mental. This will involve learning to cross-dress, leg-crossing, sit, stand, bend hair removal, wear makeup, use cosmetics, and sit down to pee.

You'll learn feminine mannerisms such as stepping daintily, arching your spine, swishing your hips, and adopting a feminine voice. You'll understand more about hormone treatment and herbal supplements.

There is advice and tips on going out in public for the first time and coming out of the closet to friends, colleagues, and family. The guide will give help you to slowly lose your masculine identity and replace it with a softer gentle feminine one.

A Collaring For A Sissy.

Collaring ceremonies are taken very seriously by the BDSM community and are tantamount to a traditional wedding. Lots of thought and planning go into such an event and can take many forms.

Mistress Anastasia's sissy maid Paula has just

completed her six months probation and has earned her collar. This is a story about Paula's service and her subsequent collaring ceremony.

The Secret Society.

Rene Glock is a freelance journalist looking for a national scoop and attempts to uncover and expose a Secret Society of Goreans which have set up residence in an old nightclub. However, as he delves into the secret world he finds he has an interest in BDSM and questions his moral right to interfere in what goes on in the Gorean Lodge.

The Good Master and Mistress Guide.

If you want to become a good Dominant and practice BDSM in a safe and considerate way, then this guide is for you.

It is written by a submissive that has had many dominants male and female over the years and knows what goes into becoming a good dominant and the mistakes some dominants make.

The book is not aimed to teach, but to make the fledgling dominant understand what is going on in the dominant-submissive dynamic, so they can understand their charges better and become better dominants.

My Transgender Journey

This is a true story with some minor alterations to protect people's identities. It is a tale about my own journey into transgender and my eventual decision to come out.

It is hoped that others can share my experiences, relate to them and perhaps take comfort from some of them.

The book has some BDSM content but is only used to put my story into context, it's about my experiences, trials and tribulations of coming out and living as a female full-time.

I hope you enjoy my little story.

Cinders

Cinders is the BDSM version of Cinderella. It is a story where an orphaned Tommy is sent to be brought up by his aunt and two very beautiful sisters.

The sisters were cruel and taunting and dressed Tommy up like a Barbie Doll. One day Tommy was caught with auntie's bra and knickers and as a punishment, he was a feminist and turned into Nancy the maid. Poor Nancy is consigned to a life of drudgery and final acceptance of life as a menial skivvy.

This story doesn't have a glass slipper or a prince, but Nancy is given a present of some new rubber gloves and a bottle of bleach. There is no happy ending or is there, you decide.

At The Races

Ryan is a hotel night porter and is at a crossroads in his life. He feels his talents are being wasted in a job with no future. Through a friend, he is offered a managerial position on a farm in Catalonia, Spain. He decides to take the post, but has no idea what sort of farm he is going to work at.

Only on the flight out to Spain, does Ryan realise that there is more to the farm than rearing chickens and growing vegetables. Later he learns the main event of the year is The Derby and there isn't a horse in sight.

I Nearly Married A Dominatrix

This is a true story that I have changed a little bit to protect people from identification. It's a story about a man's constant struggle and fights against his deep-rooted need to be submissive and a woman who conversely, is very comfortable with her dominance and heavily into the BDSM lifestyle.

They meet and get along very well indeed until Mistress Fiona announces she wants to become a professional dominatrix. Rex, the submissive boyfriend goes along with his Mistress's plans, reluctantly, but as time goes by there are more and more complications heaped on the relationship until it snaps.

Petticoat Lane.

A slightly effeminate young boy is taken under the wings of his school teacher. She becomes his guardian and trains him to become a servant girl to serve her for the rest of his life.

An unexpected incident happens and Lucy the maid has an opportunity to escape her life of drudgery and servitude, but does she take the opportunity or does she stay with her Mistress?

The Life and Times of a Victorian Maid.

This is a story about the life and times of a young Transgender who becomes a Victorian-style maid in a large exclusively B.D.S.M. household. Although fiction this story is largely based on fact, as the author herself lived in such a household for a while as a maid.

It shows the contrast between a place of safety where like-minded people can live in relative harmony and the need for ridged discipline in its serving staff.

There are many thriving households, such as the one mentioned here, tucked away out of sight and away from prying minds.

I Became a Kajira slave girl.

A Gorean scout Simon, who is looking for new talent kidnaps Emma a PhD student on sabbatical with her friend Zoey in Spain. Emma is half-drugged and sent across the ocean to the United States and ends up in the clandestine City of Gor in the Mojave desert sixty miles from civilization.

Here there is no law women are mere objects for the pleasure of men. Emma becomes a Kajira a female slave whose sole purpose in life is to please her master or be beaten tortured or killed.

Two years into Emma's servitude and she meets Simon again. Simon is consumed with guilt when he sees what Emma has been reduced to, a beaten, downtrodden and abused slave. He vows to free her from her servitude, But how they are in one of the biggest deserts in the world and sixty miles from anywhere?

Training My First Sissy Maid.

A young single mother with a part-time job, two teenage children, and up to her knees in housework is at the end of her tether and finding it harder and harder to cope.

Then reading one of her daughter's kinky magazines she found in her bedroom whilst tidying, read an article about sissy maids who are willing to work without pay just for discipline, control and structure to their lives. Excited about the prospect she decides a maid is an answer to her domestic problems.

She sets about finding a sissy to come and do her housework and be trained and moulded into becoming her loyal obedient sissy maid. On the journey she discovers she is a natural dominant and training her maid becomes a highly erotic and fulfilling experience.

A Week with Mistress Sadistic.

Susan a young female reporter in her thirties wants to know more about B.D.S.M for a future article in her magazine. She arranged to spend a week with Mistress Sadistic and watch how a professional dominatrix works.

After an eye-opening week of watching Mistress Sadistic deal with her many and varied clients, Mistress Sadistic wonders if Susan might be submissive and puts her to the text to make Susan her personal slave.

Lady Frobisher and her maid Alice.

This is a gripping tale of BDSM in Victorian England. It is a story about the lives of Lady Frobisher and her hapless maid Alice. It is a tale of lesbianism and sexual sadism with a twist at the end.

If you enjoy reading BDSM literature you'll love this as it has everything woven into an interesting tale of two people's lives at the top end of society.

K9

This is a tale that explores an area of B.D.S.M where a Mistress or Master desires a human dog (submissive) to train and treat as a real dog in every respect. Mistress Cruella is one such Mistress who takes on a young male submissive as her human dog and she takes the role of Mistress and her dog very seriously indeed.

Ryan soon becomes Max the Poodle and he struggles with his new role as a pooch but learns to be an obedient dog to please his Mistress. Max soon discovers there is far more to being a dog than meets the eye.

Bridget Monroe's Finishing School for Sissies.

Bridget and her husband are both dominant and have their own sissy maid Isabel to help them with housework. One day when the couple were on holiday in Kent, Bridget discovered an empty manor house in need of extensive repairs. On inquires, she decides to buy the manor but soon realises that to pay for the mortgage and repair costs the manor house will need to be run as a business.

Bridget used willing slaves in the B.D.S.M., community to help repair and renovate the manor house and later it was decided on advice from friends to open the manor house as a finishing school for sissies. A business had been born and later other B.D.S.M., activities were added to the core business, which included torture rooms and a medieval dungeon. Once a month an open day was held at the academy held pony races, yard sales and schoolboy classes. This also included K9 dog shows, beer tents and other amenities intending to satisfy the whole B.D.S.M., community.

Just when the business was taking off and in profit disaster struck. Society wasn't ready for Bridget Monroe's Finishing School for Sissies and Bridget was forced to close.

Printed in Great Britain
by Amazon

38243084R00089